Written and illustrated by Robert Lawson

THEY WERE STRONG AND GOOD

RABBIT HILL

AT THAT TIME

Illustrated by Robert Lawson

FERDINAND

WEE GILLIS

SIMPSON AND SAMPSON

Robbut: A Tale of Tails

ROBBUT

A Tale of Tails

BY

ROBERT LAWSON

PUBLISHED BY THE VIKING PRESS

New York · 1948

SET IN CALEDONIA AND BERNHARD MODERN BOLD TYPES
BY THE COMPOSING ROOM, INC.
AND LITHOGRAPHED IN THE UNITED STATES OF AMERICA
BY NATIONAL PROCESS COMPANY, INC.

For

MINKA

I have learned, in
whatsoever state I am,
therewith to be content.

PHILIPPIANS, II, 12

Contents

Robbut: A Tale of Tails

1. Envy

Rᴏʙʙᴜᴛ the Rabbit was, for him, quite unhappy. As a rule he was seldom unhappy and, being a young Rabbit, was never unhappy for long. But for some time now he had been getting more and more dissatisfied with his tail and this day he decided that he just couldn't stand it another minute.

By stretching his neck as long as he could and twisting his head around as far as he could, he was barely able to catch a glimpse of his tail.

It really didn't amount to much, as tails go.

"Just look at it," he muttered to himself. "Nothing but a little old tuft, that's all it is, a little old tuft of cotton. No more than a doll-baby's powder puff. And what *good* is it? What can you *do* with it? Nothing, that's what. Nothing at all."

He thought of the Cat's tail and how the Cat could lash it around when she was angry or excited, and how she could hold it up straight and proud when she was pleased. The more he thought of the Cat's tail, the more dissatisfied he became with his own.

He thought about the Cow's tail and what an excellent fly-swatter it made, and how the Squirrel used *his* bushy tail for a cape when it rained or snowed and wrapped it around his feet and nose on cold nights. There was the Possum's tail too. It certainly was not pretty, but one of the most useful of the lot. For the Possum could wrap it around a tree branch and hang there as long as he pleased. And when there were babies they could scramble up on Ma Possum's back, wrap their little tails around her big strong tail and ride there safe as could be. Yes, sir, some tails were mighty useful.

12

"A lot of use *mine* is," he grumbled. "Just a little old useless cotton tuft, that's all."

And some tails were so beautiful to look at, something really to be proud of. There was the Skunk's, for instance, plumy, shiny black with a brilliant white stripe, all arched and wavy in the breeze. The Pheasant's graceful, colorful tail feathers were lovely, and when Robbut thought about the Red Fox's tail he became really depressed and quite green with envy.

There, now, was a tail that *was* a tail! As long and almost as big around as Foxy's body. It was thick and bushy and glowing with color. Useful too. The Fox also could wrap it around his paws and bury his nose in it on cold winter nights.

Robbut stopped looking at his own useless little tail, untwisted his neck, scratched his ear disgustedly, and went on his way, most unhappy.

The path on which he was going went steeply down the hillside through a clearing that lay between two patches of pine woods. The clearing was heavily grown up in brush and Robbut was even more irritated when he had to leave the path and make his way through the brush and brambles. He knew there was a trap in the path at this point which he had to go around. All the other Animals knew it and always went round it too, so none had ever been caught, but it *was* a nuisance.

As he pushed his way through the thick tangle he suddenly heard a rattling of steel and wire and realized that someone had been caught. "Must be some stranger," he thought. "I'd better look." He squirmed his way quietly toward the sound of the rattling.

Something was caught, all right, but it was not an Animal. It was a Little Man about twenty-four inches tall, about twice what Robbut would be if he stood up on his hind legs. The Little Man seemed very angry.

The trap was a fairly large cagelike contraption of steel and wire intended to catch Animals alive without hurting them. It belonged to the Boy who lived on the hill, but as it had never caught anything the Boy had grown discouraged and seldom visited it. There was no knowing how long the Little Man might have been there. Probably

14

quite a long time, for he looked thin and unkempt and extremely irritable.

He was an old Little Man, bald, with just a thin fringe of gray hair around the back of his head and a few gray whiskers. He wore an old fashioned blue-green coat with brass buttons, knee-length trousers, and square-toed shoes with silver buckles.

Robbut had always heard that a Little Old Man lived somewhere up here on the hill, but this was the first time

15

he had ever seen him. He hopped cautiously up to the cage and asked politely, "Is there anything I can do?"

"Of course there is," the Little Old Man snapped. "You can get me out of this confounded affair. That is, if you've got any sense, which I doubt. Rabbits not noted for it. Knew your grandfather—he had just a little sense. Know your father—he has considerably less. Now you—even less, probably. A little divided by two, divided by three, doesn't leave much, does it?"

Robbut admitted that it didn't, but he did try hard to get the cage open. He kicked and butted and banged at it, making no progress at all.

"Look, boy," said the Little Man after a few minutes of this, "stop using your head for a hammer and try to think with it a bit. Now, do you see this heavy steel wire across here? Just lift that up all the way to the top and the end will come open and I can get out."

So Robbut concentrated on the steel wire. He managed to lift it up a little with his forepaws, then he got his nose under it and lifted it still higher. Then it slipped and dropped down again.

"Your fingers are all thumbs," the Little Old Man said, "or your paws are all feet or something. Anyway, hand me a twig." So Robbut gave him a twig, and now each time that the heavy steel catch was raised a bit the Little Man stuck the twig through the wire mesh and held it there. After some time they managed to get it almost to the top of the cage, at which point the twig broke and the heavy wire dropped again, this time on Robbut's paw.

"Ouch!" he cried, rubbing the paw. "If I only had a tail like the Possum's I could sit up on the top of the cage and let my tail down and lift that thing up just as easy as anything."

"Well you haven't and you can't," the Little Old Man snapped. "Give me another twig—a stouter one."

Robbut gave him a stronger twig and went to work again. He pushed and strained and shoved and this time when the heavy wire had almost reached the top of the cage he turned around quickly and gave it a good strong kick. Kicking was one thing he was really good at. The

wire flew up over the top, the door opened, and the Little Old Man stepped out.

"Well," he said, dusting off his hands, "that's that, and a fine mess it was. Should have known better, at my age, than to go fooling around with any such dangerous contraption as that, but I wanted to see how it worked and I certainly found out."

"Were you in there long, sir?" Robbut asked.

"Two days," answered the Little Man. "Two days and three nights, without a bit of food or drink or even a smoke. Come on, I'm famished."

He darted into the brush and made his way up the hill so rapidly that Robbut had difficulty following him. When they arrived at the foot of a big tree on the edge of the Pine Wood the Little Man paused and looked all round

carefully. Then he grasped a loose-looking piece of bark between two of the roots and gave it a pull. It was really a cleverly hinged little door which, when opened, revealed a short flight of steps.

Down these the Little Old Man plunged eagerly, shouting over his shoulder, "Wipe your feet, and close the door, and lock it—and hurry. I'm *starving*."

2. Ecstasy

B Y THE time Robbut had wiped his feet carefully, locked the door, and gone down the steps, the Little Old Man had a fire started in the stove and was busily rummaging in various cabinets. He got out a bowl of strawberries, half a dozen eggs, some strips of bacon, coffee, butter, cream, biscuits, sugar, and all the other things necessary for a hearty breakfast. Finally he discovered a bunch of carrots and tossed them to Robbut.

"That's probably your idea of a breakfast," he chuckled. "Personally I can do with something more solid." He broke five eggs into a now sizzling pan and laid in six strips of bacon.

Robbut thanked him politely for the carrots and nibbled on one while he looked around at the Little Old Man's home. It certainly was a cozy place, much bigger than any burrow he'd ever been in and much better furnished. There were lots of comfortable chairs, a built-in bed, tables, and a desk. There were innumerable chests, cabinets, cupboards, and shelves, all filled with books, china, food, and various interesting-looking things. The chimney ran up into the hollow trunk of the big tree so the smoke could not be noticed from outside, and the small curtained windows looked out through well-concealed openings in the roots and stumps. Robbut had passed this tree dozens of times and never dreamed that anyone lived under it.

The Little Old Man was far too busy eating now to talk, so Robbut nibbled at his carrots and waited politely for him to finish. After a while the eggs and bacon and biscuits *and* strawberries were demolished. The Little Man groaned comfortably, loosened his belt, and sank into an easy chair to enjoy his third cup of coffee. He filled and lit his pipe, blew out a great cloud of smoke, and smiled most kindly at Robbut.

"Well, young man," he said, "you did real well with that trap, real well—for a Rabbit. Very willing and quite smart —for a Rabbit, of course. I certainly am obliged, most grateful and all that. I'm deeply indebted to you and when I'm indebted to anyone I like to do something about it. Always believe in paying my debts and this is a really big one. Now, what can I do for you?"

"Oh, I don't know," Robbut answered. "I—I guess I'd like another carrot."

The Little Man tossed him another carrot and snorted indignantly, "A *carrot!* So that's all you think I'm worth! Here you saved my life and I ask you to name a worthy reward and you say a carrot! That's stupid—even for a Rabbit—and downright insulting. A carrot indeed!"

"Oh goodness, I didn't mean it that way," Robbut cried hastily, "I just couldn't think."

"Well, suppose you try," the Little Man said, more kindly. "What would you like more than anything in the world?"

Robbut thought and thought, while he nibbled at the carrot. For a while he couldn't think of anything, then suddenly he remembered about his tail.

"Well," he said hesitantly, "the only thing I can think of that I want terribly is a new tail—but of course you can't do anything about that."

"That's what *you* think," said the Little Man. "But what's the matter with your present one? Looks all right to me—for a Rabbit."

"Oh, it's just a little old tuft," answered Robbut, "just a little old cotton tuft—and you can't *do* anything with it."

"You can twitch it," the Little Man said.

"Yes—a little," Robbut admitted, "but not much—not to amount to anything." And he went on to describe how all the other Animals could *do* things with their tails, how they could express their feelings with them, how useful

23

they were, and how beautiful. "All I can do with *mine* is sit on it," he concluded miserably.

The Little Old Man, who had listened attentively, puffed his pipe and considered the problem a while.

"Well," he finally said, "there's something in what you say. Personally, of course, I wouldn't give it a thought, *but*, if you want a new tail, you want a new tail, and that's that. What kind of a tail do you want?"

Robbut thought until he had finished the carrot. "I think," he said at last, "I think a Cat's tail would be nice."

"What kind of a Cat?"

"Well, black maybe—with a white tip, or perhaps Maltese?"

"If it was mine," said the Little Man, "I'd take a stripedy one, a nice warm gray with dark stripes and a real black tip. However, it's *your* tail, choose your own colors. While you're doing that, suppose you wash up the dishes and I'll figure this out."

So Robbut gathered up all the dishes and pans and coffee cups and washed them carefully in the little stone sink. There were a good many of them and there was quite a lot of bacon grease and egg, so it took some time to get them all done and neatly put away in the cupboard. He thought hard about the different colored tails and finally decided that a gray striped one would be nicest.

While he was doing this the Little Old Man busied around, getting down dusty jars and bottles and boxes

from different shelves and consulting many queer old books and papers. He grouped up all sorts of odd-looking things in a little mortar and at last put them all into a stone jug which was placed on the stove to warm. The jar gave out a strange but not unpleasant odor.

"There now," he said, washing his hands and polishing his spectacles. "That ought to do it. Grandfather used to do a good deal of this sort of thing, but I'm pretty rusty at it. Now then," he said to Robbut, who had just hung up the dishtowel, "hop up here on the table and listen carefully."

Robbut did and the Little Man went on, "Now close

your eyes tight and put your paws over them—no peeking—and hold perfectly still—"

"Will it hurt?" Robbut asked anxiously.

"Not in the least, but *do* hold still. Be a fine mess if it came out crooked or in the wrong place or something."

So Robbut closed his eyes tightly, put his forepaws over them, and held perfectly still, although his heart was bumping rather hard with excitement. He could feel his little tufty tail being gently twisted and pulled and rubbed. He felt something warm and sticky being put on it and could smell the peculiar odor that had come from the stone pot on the stove.

Then all of a sudden he felt a slap on his back and the Little Man shouted, "Fine, fine. All done. Take a look at it."

Robbut took down his paws and opened his eyes. He stretched his neck as far as he could and twisted his head as far as he could—and almost collapsed with joy and surprise. For there, rising sleek and proud and curving from his rear end, was the handsomest Cat's tail that anyone could imagine!

"Oh, my goodness," he gasped. "*Isn't* it beautiful."

"It's all right," the Little Man agreed. "Came out very well indeed. Quite proud of it myself. Here, here's a mirror."

He put an old mirror on the floor and leaned it against the wall. Robbut viewed himself and his new tail from

26

every possible angle. The more he looked the greater were his pride and joy. He strode past with his tail straight up, quivering with pleasure, just the tip of it swaying slightly. He lashed it as though he were angry until it pounded his ribs and raised clouds of dust from the rug. He lay down and waved it in slow, stately, pleased circles. He swung it around until it tickled his chin and he could stroke it with his forepaws. He did everything with it a Cat could do and some things only a Rabbit would think of.

"Oh, my," he finally breathed. "It's the most beautiful tail in all the world. I can't *tell* you how grateful I am."

"It *is* a very handsome tail," chuckled the Little Old Man "—for a Cat. For a Rabbit—I don't know. Looks a bit odd. Well, anyway, see how it works out. Remember, if you don't like it you can always bring it back and change it."

"Little chance of that." Robbut laughed happily. He was dying to show himself off to all his friends and relations, so he hastily thanked the Little Old Man again, raced up the steps, and burst out into the sunlight. Then he gave a shrill shriek of pain, for he had forgotten the length of his new tail and had slammed the door on it—hard.

3. Difficulty

THE NEW tail hurt frightfully and Robbut tried to lick it the way he had always seen Cats lick theirs when they got hurt. But not having the currycomb sort of tongue that Cats have it didn't seem to do much good; the fur just got wet and slimy. So he rubbed it with his paws for a while and soon it felt better, but it didn't look so handsome. The tip was quite swollen and the wet fur was not at all attractive.

However, he walked on down the path waving his tail proudly. and twisting his head around now and then to admire it. Soon he spied some Grasshoppers and stalked them the way a Cat would. He flattened himself on the ground with his chin stretched out and his tail straight in the grass, just the tip twitching a bit. Then he would inch up very, very slowly and finally make a great spring, with his tail stuck straight up in the air.

The Grasshoppers just hopped out of the way and jeered, "Lookat Robbut, Lookat Robbut. Trying to be a Cat, Trying to be a Cat!" over and over again. It was fun though, and Robbut enjoyed it—for a while. He lashed his tail and acted very fierce, but the Grasshoppers just continued to chant, "Lookat Robbut, Lookat Robbut," which finally became quite tiresome.

There was some trouble with the new tail too. Lashing it around in the grass this way it began to pick up all sorts of things. First one or two burdock burrs caught in it, then some devil's pitchforks, then a lot of beggar lice. There were bits of dry grass and quite a few pine needles. The handsome tail was beginning to look quite messy. Robbut tried switching and shaking it, but that didn't do any good. Then he tried licking it, but that just made it wetter and messier. Then he tried biting out the burrs

the way Cats did, but he wasn't very good at that. He pulled out several tufts of fur and finally bit himself quite painfully.

He decided that he'd better get along down the hill and show off his new tail while it still looked like something. But he had barely started when there was a loud s-w-o-o-s-h and a harsh clanging shriek as a Bluejay sailed just over his head. A second later another one dove at him from the opposite direction. Then three Crows arrived, and while one stationed himself in a treetop and squawked out a perfect fire alarm the other two joined the Bluejays in diving and flapping around poor Robbut.

He yelled as loudly as he could, "I'm not a Cat—I'm Robbut the Rabbit," but the racket was now so deafening that no one could hear him. He couldn't even hear himself, and when two pairs of Robins arrived and joined in,

no one could hear anything. All that the Birds could see
of him in the deep grass was his long striped tail and it
certainly was a Cat's tail. They didn't like Cats and they
told the whole countryside so.

Robbut continued to make his way down the hillside

as best he could, for he was still determined to show himself off to his friends and relations. But he realized that there was not much chance of that now. He knew that the moment one of these Bird alarms started every Little Animal on the hill would begin to rush around and squeal, "Cat's on the prowl, Cat's on the prowl!" He knew that within a matter of minutes they would all be deep down in their burrows with the doors tightly closed.

But he kept on, because there didn't seem to be anything else to do. The Jays and the Crows made more and more noise and swooped closer and closer to him. They were bolder now because he didn't stand up and bat at them as a Cat would. One Jay took a good nip out of his tail and a Crow whanged his nose with its wing.

He finally reached his own home, but as he had feared, there was no one around and everything was shut up tight. He pounded and called, "Mother, Father, it's Robbut, let me in," but no one could possibly have heard him. He went to his uncle's burrow where all his cousins lived, the cousins to whom he had especially wanted to show off. That was closed too and no one was around. The Fieldmice and Chipmunks and Squirrels had all disappeared, even the Skunks and Woodchucks.

About this time the Lady who lived in the Big House on the hill noticed the racket and called to the Boy, "Son, there's a strange Cat out there bothering the Birds. See if you can't chase it away."

34

The Boy, the same one who owned the trap, gathered up a collection of good throwing stones and went to look. He could see a stripedy Cat's tail moving around in the field so he began to throw stones at it. He didn't try to hit it, just to come as close as he could and scare it away.

As the first stone landed close beside him Robbut leaped to the left. Then one bounced over him and

another fell just in front of him, so he doubled back.
Another whipped through the grass on his right side and
he ran to the left. One thumped on his left and he leaped to
the right. Back and forth across the field he raced, becoming more and more confused and more and more tired.

The Crows and Jays and Robins retired to a distance
when the stone throwing began, which was some relief,

but the tail was becoming a great nuisance. It was filled with burrs and trash and kept getting caught in briars, which pulled out great tufts of fur.

Robbut slowly managed to work his way up the hill toward the brushy clearing where the Little Man's house was. The stones gradually stopped dropping and the Birds had gone away, all but one Crow who perched on the tip top of a pine tree and occasionally uttered a dismal croak.

It was almost evening now. There was a chilly east wind and it was beginning to drizzle. Robbut got colder and wetter and hungrier and more unhappy. The swelling on his tail where the door had slammed on it was aching and the spot where the Bluejay had gashed it throbbed painfully.

He dragged himself wearily up to the Little Old Man's house and there on the door hung a small sign which read:

NAPPING—DO NOT DISTURB.

Exhausted and miserable, Robbut crept under a bush and burrowed into the wet leaves. The east wind grew colder, the drizzle drizzled harder, and his tail throbbed worse and worse.

4. Pride

Rᴏʙʙᴜᴛ was waked by brilliant sun flickering in his eyes. The rain had stopped and it was a beautiful warm morning, fresh and bursting with life. But Robbut was neither warm nor fresh and he certainly was not bursting with life. He was cold and damp and stiff; every

joint and muscle ached. He was hungry—and as for his tail, it was just a mess. It was wet and swollen and muddy and full of burrs and trash. It hurt so badly that he didn't even try to stir it, he just let it lie limply on the wet ground.

He was trying to rub the sleep out of his eyes and stretch a little of the stiffness out of his joints when a young Garter Snake came slithering along. He had just shed his old skin and was filled with energy and pride of his shiny new coat. It *was* very beautiful, with its glistening, almost black scales and its three bright yellow stripes.

"Goodness gracious, Robbut!" he cried, "whatever's happened to you, and what's wrong with your tail, or whoever's tail it is? It can't be yours, but it seems to be on you. It looks like a Cat's, but no Cat would have that mussy a tail. What's this all about anyway?"

Robbut rather sheepishly explained about it; how he had saved the Little Old Man from the trap and how the Little Old Man had given him a new tail.

"Well, I must say you made an awfully poor choice," exclaimed the Snake. "Of all the stupid things I've ever heard, that's about the stupidest—even for a Rabbit. What would anyone, especially *you*, want with a long furry nuisance like that?

"Now there—" and he twitched his own tail in the sunshine—"there's what *I* call a tail. It's clean cut, useful, no trouble, and if I do say so, quite handsome. What's more, it will never get muddy, stained, or spotted—or stuck up with burrs or pine needles. Sheds water like a Duck and has real life and style to it."

His tail, flickering and quivering in the sunshine, really did look most attractive and extremely lively. It certainly was neat and clean. Robbut eyed it with envy and his unfortunate tail with regret.

"I—I think I *would* like one like that," he said.

"Almost anything would be better than that mess you've got there," laughed the Snake. "Why don't you ask the Little Man for one?" He went slithering off down the path, still laughing.

At this moment the Little Old Man came out of his door. He looked about approvingly at the bright sunshine, stretched, yawned, and took down the DO NOT DISTURB sign. He was about to go in again when he caught sight of poor Robbut.

"Heavenly ·dustbins!" he exclaimed. "What has happened to you?"

"Almost everything," Robbut exclaimed sadly. He started to explain, but the Little Man interrupted him.

"Come in, come in," he cried, "before my bacon gets cold. Get warm and dried out and get some breakfast inside you—then you can tell me all about it."

The room was warm and cozy, with a lovely odor of hot biscuits and coffee and bacon and tobacco smoke. The Little Man pushed a chair up close to the stove and told Robbut to sit in it. Then he brought out a bunch of carrots, half a head of crisp lettuce, and an apple. Robbut had not realized how hungry he was but he did now and pitched in ravenously, while the Little Man finished his

bacon and eggs and coffee. By the time their breakfasts were eaten Robbut was well dried out, thoroughly warm, and much more cheerful. For a while last night he had thought that he would rather have his old tail back, but now that he felt better he was eager to experiment with a new one.

The Little Old Man laughed heartily at the sad tale of yesterday's troubles. "I thought it was a mistake," he chuckled, "thought it was a foolish choice—even for a Rabbit. Well, what would you like to try now?"

Robbut told him of his talk with the Garter Snake and of all the advantages of a Snake's tail. He guessed he'd like to try one of those if the Little Man didn't mind.

"Well, there's something in what you say," the Little Man admitted. "It *would* be clean and sanitary. What kind of a Snake's tail do you want; Blacksnake, Garter

Snake, Milk Snake, Moccasin, King Snake, Rattlesnake? Take your choice. A Rattlesnake's might be fun. You could rattle your rattles and frighten the daylights out of your friends and relations."

"I don't think that would be a good idea," said Robbut thoughtfully "—even for a Rabbit. Mother and Father are going to be angry anyway over my being out all night and if I frightened the daylights—no, I think a Garter Snake would be best."

"Well, it's *your* tail," the Little Man agreed. "And if you want a Snake's tail, you want a Snake's tail and that's that. But there's one thing more. Just what *is* a Snake's tail? I mean where does it begin and where does it stop? I'd say it started just back of his ears, if he had ears. As I see it a Snake's practically *all* tail—"

"It shouldn't be *too* long," Robbut said. "That would be awkward. I'd think, just about as long as I am."

"Very well," said the Little Man. "Hop up here and I'll see what I can do. Close your eyes tight and put your paws over them—and no peeking."

The stone crock had been warming on the stove, so now Robbut hopped up on the table, closed his eyes, and put

his forepaws over them. He could smell the strange odor again and feel the pain and throbbing of his Cat's tail slowly disappear. Then suddenly the Little Old Man was slapping him on the back and shouting, "Fine, fine. Take a look!"

Robbut stretched his neck and twisted his head and there was the *most* beautiful Garter Snake's tail, even handsomer than the one he had seen this morning. It was sleek, black, and shining, with three beautiful golden stripes running its full length. It seemed to quiver and twitch and wriggle with life and energy. He swung it around and tickled his ear with it. He stroked its shiny smoothness with his forepaws.

"Oh, my goodness," he cried. "This is *certainly* the most wonderful tail in the world."

RL

"Not bad, not at all bad," the Little Old Man agreed. "A little longer than I intended, but not bad at all."

"I can't tell you how grateful I am," Robbut said.

The Little Man lit his pipe and settled in a comfortable chair. "You can *show* me," he chuckled.

So Robbut gathered up all the breakfast dishes and washed and dried them. It was fun now, for Robbut could wind his new tail around the cup handles and whisk the cups up into the cupboard or pick up the forks and spoons and drop them into the drawers as easily as could be. When he had finished he dried and polished his tail with the dishtowel and hung that neatly on the rack.

"Very useful and very handsome," said the Little Old Man. "Now run along and show it off to your friends and relations. I know you're dying to, but *do* try to keep out of trouble. And remember, if it doesn't work you can always come back and change it."

Robbut thanked him again and dashed up the steps. This time he flicked his tail up over his back and didn't slam the door on it.

5. Disgrace

Rᴏʙʙᴜᴛ went gaily down the hill, filled with pride and vainglory. He passed the Grasshoppers that he had stalked yesterday, but when they began to jeer "Lookat Robbut, Lookat Robbut," he flicked out with his new tail and sent the largest one spinning ten feet through the air.

47

A Fly lit on Robbut's back and he smacked him just as easily as he had the Grasshopper. "This is a *useful* tail," he thought. Then for a while, as he hopped along, he amused himself by snapping the heads off daisies. He practiced cracking his tail like a whip and soon was able to make quite a loud crack. "This tail is *fun* too," he thought. "I guess I'm the first Rabbit in the world that was ever able to crack his tail like a coach whip. Wait 'til Cousin Harold sees it, I bet he'll be jealous." Cousin Harold was somewhat older than Robbut and always lorded it over him a bit.

Robbut finally reached his uncle's burrow and found his cousins playing around in the field. He ran up to greet them, proudly snapping his new tail. They all stopped their play and gathered around him, astonished, but not greatly impressed, especially Cousin Harold.

"Where'd you get that old Rat's tail?" he demanded. "It makes you look just like a Rat."

"It does not," Robbut answered indignantly, "and it's not a Rat's tail. It's a Garter Snake's tail. Look." He lowered it on the ground and it wriggled around in the grass exactly like a Garter Snake. One or two of the little girl cousins screamed and ran, but Harold leaped high in the air and came down *kerthump* on the beautiful new tail.

"*Ouch!*" screeched Robbut. The pain brought tears to his eyes and he held his tail high up, out of harm's way.

48

"I can do all sorts of things with it that you can't," he said, after the pain had subsided a bit. He flicked out his tail and neatly snipped off the head of a daisy.

"Aw, that's nothing," Harold scoffed. He leaped high over a daisy and just as neatly kicked off a flower with his hind feet.

"You can't do it with your *tail*," Robbut said.

"Who wants to?" said Harold.

"I can tickle my ear with my tail; you can't do that," Robbut boasted.

Harold didn't even answer him, but just flopped his right ear over and tickled it with his hind foot.

"Well, anyway it's beautiful," Robbut said, wriggling and flicking his shiny tail in the sunlight.

"Beautiful like a Rat," Harold scoffed. Then he started to jeer, "Robbut the Rat! Robbut the Rat!"

The other cousins joined in and they all hopped around

in a circle, chanting, "Robbut the Rat! Robbut the Rat!"

The Skunk and the Woodchuck, attracted by the racket, came over to see what was going on.

"Well, for Heaven's sake," exclaimed the Skunk, "if you were getting a new tail why didn't you get a *good* one?" and proudly waved his own beautiful black-and-white tail in the air.

"I—guess I didn't think," Robbut admitted.

"Humph," snorted the Woodchuck. "Some people are never satisfied. What are your Ma and Pa going to say to this?"

"I didn't think about that either," Robbut answered uneasily.

"Well, you'd better," the Woodchuck grunted and waddled away.

Robbut did begin to think then and the more he thought the more uneasy he became. He knew that his parents would not be pleased over his staying away all

night and now he began to suspect that they might be even less pleased with his new tail.

He guessed he'd better find out, so he pushed his way through the circle of still chanting cousins. "You're just jealous, that's all," he yelped at Cousin Harold and snapped him on the nose with his tail. The cousins followed him for a while, still jeering, "Robbut the Rat! Robbut the Rat!" but they finally got tired of that and went off to do something else.

As he approached his home burrow, Mother came rushing out to meet him. "Oh, Robbut darling," she cried, "we have been *so* worried. Where have you—?" She suddenly stopped and turned pale as she caught sight of his new tail. "Oh, Son," she gasped, "what has happened to you? What is that awful thing?" Then she started to weep.

Father had come out and was looking at Robbut in horror. Finally he spoke.

"This," he said, "is the most crushing blow that has ever happened to me. From time to time certain malicious gossips have spread the rumor that there was a strain of Rat blood in our family. This I have always

vigorously denied and have managed to squelch all such vile suspicions. Now *you* must appear—obviously part Rat! Oh, the disgrace! Oh, the humiliation!

"Go!" he shouted. "Go, and never darken our door again!"

"But it's *not*," Robbut cried. "It's *not* a Rat's tail; it's a Snake's tail, a Garter Snake's tail. The Little Old Man gave it to me." He tried to tell them about it, but Father interrupted.

"A likely tale," he scoffed. "And a loathsome tail. *Go!*" he roared. Mother wept harder and took a step toward him, but Father held her back. "*Go!*" he roared again.

Robbut went.

His tail dragged along behind him. He didn't feel like snapping off daisies with it now, or flicking it in the sun. He was getting hungry too and thought sadly of the appetizing lunch Mother would be preparing—as soon as she had stopped weeping.

He stopped and ate a little clover, but it didn't set very well. He was beginning to feel that his new tail was not a great success. He was tired too, he hadn't slept much the night before.

A Bluejay settled in a near-by tree and began to yawp, "Robbut the Rat. Robbut the Rat."

"Oh, shut up," Robbut snapped. He crawled under a bush and settled down for a nap.

It just happened that the bush he had chosen was right beside a footpath that wandered up the hill. And it also just happened that when Robbut flopped down for his nap his long shining Snake's tail was stretched clear across the path.

The sun was warm and Robbut slept soundly, but along toward the middle of the afternoon Frank Glynn came walking up the path. He had a spade over his shoulder for he was going to spade up the garden of the Big House on the hill.

Now Frank was a perfectly nice kind-hearted fellow who wouldn't hurt anybody, but he did have a horror of Snakes. So when he suddenly almost stepped on what

looked like quite a large Snake the spade just seemed to fly off his shoulder and he gave the Snake a good healthy chop.

Robbut woke screeching with pain, made a six-foot leap from under the bush and streaked up the hill, leaving his Snake's tail wriggling in the dust of the path.

"Heavenly Peter!" exclaimed Frank. "And what would that be?" He looked under the bush for the rest of the Snake, but there was nothing there. "Well, strange things

do happen," he muttered, scratching his head. He kicked the tail out of the path and went on up the hill about his business.

Robbut went flying up through the brushy clearing toward the Little Old Man's house. His tail, or where his tail had been, burned like a hot coal of fire. This time he didn't even notice whether or not there was a sign on the Little Man's door. He snatched it open, tumbled down the steps, and burst screeching into the living room, where the Little Man had just lit his after-luncheon pipe.

While Robbut, crying *"Ouch, Ouch, Ouch,"* rushed round and round the room, the Little Old Man got up,

went over to the stove, and picked up the stone crock.

"Had this heating," he said with a grin. "Thought you'd probably be needing it. Come now, hop up on the table and close your eyes—and no peeking."

Robbut leaped up on the table and crouched down, sobbing and trembling. He smelled the strange but not unpleasant odor from the stone crock and suddenly felt the terrible pain ease and gradually disappear.

Then the Little Old Man was saying, "Well, what kind of a tail do you want *now*?"

"My—own—I guess," sighed Robbut. "If you don't mind."

He smelled the strange odor again and felt a warm feeling where his tail should be. Then the Little Man slapped him on the back and cried, "There you are. Same as ever. Same old tail. Take a look."

Robbut stretched his neck as far as he could and twisted his head as far as he could and was able to just catch a glimpse of his little old tufty tail. It looked pretty good.

The Little Old Man gave him a stout supper of pea-vine soup, carrots, and lettuce. Then he said, "Come now, you've had a couple of hard days and nights. Better get a nice long sleep.'

Robbut hopped up into an extra bunk, the Little Man covered him with a patchwork quilt, and he immediately fell into a deep slumber.

6. Vainglory

ROBBUT slept soundly until the next morning, when the Little Old Man waked him and gave him a good hearty breakfast. Robbut felt well rested, much refreshed, and, for the time being, quite satisfied with his own tail.

"Now then," said the Little Man, after Robbut had

59

done the dishes, "I hope you're going to be contented and leave well enough alone—but I doubt it. If you do feel like more experimenting, come in any time. Right now you'd better hop along and make your peace with your family."

"Thank you ever so much," Robbut said, "and I don't think I'll want to try any more tails."

"You don't today," the Little Man laughed, "but that doesn't mean you won't tomorrow. You haven't much of a memory—even for a Rabbit."

Robbut hopped happily down the hill. It was really quite a relief to have his little old compact tail back again. It felt much lighter than the Cat's tail and it certainly couldn't get him into the troubles that the Snake's tail had.

When he approached the cousins they started to jeer, "Robbut the Rat! Robbut the Rat!" but he gave Harold a good kick in the ribs and ran on home, affording them all a clear view of his white cottony tail.

Mother greeted Robbut with tears of joy, but Father regarded him with some suspicion. He walked round him several times, inspecting his tail closely.

"I am much relieved," he finally said, "to find that this was just a temporary phase, although a most unfortunate one. It must never happen again."

Robbut explained to them about the Little Old Man and how he had given him two new tails.

"I recollect clearly the Cat scare," Father said. "It caused us a great deal of worry and inconvenience. Your choice of a Snake's tail was still more thoughtless—even for a *young* Rabbit. I hope you have learned your lesson well and will cause us no further concern or humiliation. I trust that you will be contented with the appendage which Nature and inheritance originally gave you. After all, a Rabbit's tail is nothing to be ashamed of."

"No, sir, yes, sir," Robbut answered dutifully, and went in to get some more breakfast.

61

For at least two days he was well contented with his old tail. He helped Mother around the burrow and played with his cousins and fought with Cousin Harold most happily, without ever giving a thought to his tail.

By the third day, however, he had completely forgotten about his troubles with the Cat's tail and by the fourth day he had completely forgotten about his painful experiences with the Snake's tail. His memory, as the Little Man had said, was not at all good—even for a Rabbit. By the fifth day he was again becoming dissatisfied with his own tail and on the sixth day he met the Red Fox.

To see the Red Fox's tail was really something thrilling. It was thick and soft, orange-red on top, shading to a rich creamy white underneath, and almost as long and as round as the Fox himself.

"Goodness, Mr. Fox," Robbut said admiringly, "I guess you have about the most beautiful tail in the world."

"Well, I don't know," Foxy answered modestly,

waving his tail back and forth. "There *may* be handsomer ones or more useful ones in the world, but I've just never happened to see any."

"Is yours useful?" inquired Robbut.

"Is it *useful*?" said the Fox. Why you take a cold winter night and you can wrap it around over all your paws and bury your nose in it and sleep as warm as a bug in a rug."

"I think I'd love to have a tail like that," Robbut sighed.

"I don't doubt it," the Red Fox laughed. "Who wouldn't? But just try and get one."

"I guess I will," Robbut said and wandered up the hill toward the Little Old Man's house.

"My, my," chuckled the Little Man as he answered Robbut's knock and let him in. "Six whole days without a new tail. You're learning a *little* sense—for a Rabbit, but I thought you'd be back. What is it now?"

"Fox tail," Robbut burst out. "I just *must* have a Fox tail. They're *so* beautiful—and useful too. I *must* have one."

"Well," the Little Man said thoughtfully, "there's something in what you say. On Foxes they are undoubtedly handsome; I have even seen them on Ladies and on the front of motorcycles and trucks going by on the road, and they don't look badly there. But on a Rabbit—I don't know. However, it's your tail, and if you want a Fox tail, you want a Fox tail—and that's that. Come now. Hop up, close your eyes, and no peeking."

Robbut smelled the now familiar odor from the stone crock, he felt the warm feeling on his rear end and then the slap on the back. He heard the Little Old Man crying, "There you are. Take a look, take a look."

He didn't even have to stretch his neck or twist his head very far this time. He could, by just turning his head slightly, see the most beautiful, soft, plumy, orangey-creamy tail that anyone ever had—especially a Rabbit.

"Oh my!" he gasped. "Did you ever *see* anything more beautiful?"

"Yes," said the Little Man. "I've seen lots of things

64

more beautiful. But as a tail it *is* extremely handsome— for a Fox. For you—I don't know. But, you wanted a Fox tail and you've got a Fox tail—and that's that. Now run along. I've planned a nice long nap for myself this afternoon."

Robbut wandered around the Pine Wood in a daze of pride and happiness. He couldn't *do* as many things with this tail as with his other tails, but it was *so* beautiful! He spent so much time with his head twisted around looking at it that his neck began to get quite stiff. So he went down by the river where there was a quiet pool which made an excellent mirror. Here he spent the entire afternoon posing and admiring himself.

He paced slowly back and forth with his plumy tail
stretched straight out, just curved up a little at the end.
He sat down and waved it gently, like a fan. Then he sat

up proudly and curled it around his feet, so that he looked like a china animal with a beautiful orangey base. He ran back and forth so it streamed and rippled along behind him. He kept this up until it grew too dark

to see his reflection, and all the time he grew prouder and more pleased with himself and his new tail.

He didn't quite dare go home, for although no one could possibly call this a Rat's tail or accuse him of looking like a Rat, he still wasn't quite sure just how Father would take it, beautiful as it was. So he picked out a spot up near the Pine Wood that was nice and clean and dry, where his proud new tail could not possibly get soiled. Here he lay down to spend the night. He remembered what the Fox had said about curling his tail around over his feet and burying his nose in it. Of course that was for cold winter nights and this happened to be a warm autumn night, but Robbut tried it anyway. At first it was wonderfully snug and cozy, but soon it became oppressively hot. Robbut slept very badly and kept waking up. Finally, along toward morning, he uncurled his tail and stretched it out behind him. This was more comfortable and he soon fell into a heavy slumber.

From this he was rudely wakened by the baying of the Hounds of the Swallowtail Hunt.

7. Tribulation

Robbut came awake at once and peeped out through the trees. Down in the lower field he could see the pack of Hounds and many horses and riders, some of them in bright red coats. They were all boiling into the field through a gate on the road.

"I think," said Robbut to himself, "that I'd better be somewhere else." He turned hastily, but as he did so his beautiful orangey tail must have shone in the sunlight and caught the eye of some Hound or huntsman. For at once the baying of the Hounds rose to excited screaming yelps. There were shouts from the riders, the thin notes of the Huntsman's horn and a long call of *"Gone Aw-a-a-a-y."*

"I think," said Robbut to himself, "that I'd better be somewhere else *real soon."* He streaked through the Pine Wood and down through the brushy clearing while the whole Swallowtail Hunt came thundering up the other side of the hill.

Robbut was not especially worried, for he knew just about every trick there is for getting rid of Dogs. He knew every thicket and briar patch and barbed wire fence in these parts and just how to dodge through them, leaving the Dogs hung up in the briars or wire. He knew all the streams and just where they were shallow enough to cross or narrow enough to jump, which would usually throw a Dog off the scent. Right now he was making for the ford in the river. Here the stream was shallow and there were some big stones which made crossing quite easy.

He knew also that the Swallowtail Hounds were carefully trained not to follow the trails of Rabbits, but only those of Foxes. Thinking of this, a sudden horrible possibility occurred to him. "Goodness," he thought, "do you suppose my Fox's tail will leave a Fox's scent? It probably will. This is serious!"

Evidently it did, for as he crossed the river road he could hear the screaming pack hot and true on his trail, tearing down through the brushy clearing. The riders had gone around through a cleared field and he could hear the thundering of the horses somewhere to his left.

The stones in the ford were quite far apart, but Robbut had hopped across them many times. This time however, what with his haste and the unaccustomed weight of the new tail, which somewhat upset his balance, he skidded across the last stone and plunged into the icy water.

The water was shallow and he was close to the bank, so he managed to scramble out quickly. The unfortunate thing was that the beautiful plumy tail got soaking wet and absorbed several pounds of water. As he clawed his way up the bank and into the bushes it's weight was a terrible handicap. It was like having a bag of sand tied to his rear end.

He got into the shelter of the bushes and started upstream just in time, for a moment later the Hounds burst out of the clearing and the riders all came galloping up the road. They met at the ford, and as Robbut went around a curve in the river bank far upstream he could see a scene of considerable confusion. Horses were splashing around in the shallow water, Hounds were all over the place, and the Huntsman was blowing his horn wildly.

They had lost the trail, for the moment, and Robbut

could ease up a little. It was high time too, for the weight of his water-soaked tail was most exhausting. He shook it as much as he could and it gradually dried out a bit and became somewhat lighter, but not much.

The river was bordered by bushes and Robbut, staying in the cover of these, went far upstream. He crossed the river at another shallow spot, continued on the near side until he came to a bridge, and again crossed over. This, he thought, should have pretty well confused his trail. He gave a great sigh of relief, for he was now close to the huge briar patch that he had been making for all the time. It was several acres in extent and he knew every path and runway in it. It was, he knew, completely Dog-proof.

Just as he reached it he heard the pack in full cry

again, coming up the river road toward the bridge. "You're too late," he laughed, plunging into the nearest tunnel, "I fooled you that time."

His laugh changed to a yip of pain as he made another horrifying discovery. The beautiful plumy tail was caught in the briars. With a sinking feeling he realized that he could no more get into the briar patch with that tail than he could with an umbrella. He backed out hastily and yanked free, leaving several handfuls of orange fur hanging on the thorns.

He knew now that his only hope lay in running; running far and fast. He circled the briar patch and set off through a pasture just as the Swallowtail Hunt came clattering over the bridge. He was in clear view and could hear the Hounds' voices rise and the Huntsman's horn and the shouts of the riders. He didn't pay much attention to them though—he just ran.

Ordinarily Robbut was a good runner, one of the best in the county. Ordinarily he could have outdistanced these bellowing Hounds and silly riders with the greatest of ease. He would have rather enjoyed it—ordinarily. But with the handicap of this tail it was an entirely different affair. Even though the thing had dried out it was still a terrific drag.

For a moment he thought longingly of his little old streamlined tufty tail, but he didn't have much time for thinking. He was too busy running.

He ran up through pastures and over stone walls. He ran down through cornfields and wheatfields and hayfields and woodlots. He jumped fences and streams and ditches, but always the screaming pack drew closer and the thunder of the Horses grew nearer, the tail dragged more and more heavily.

Robbut was about done.

He was in strange and unfamiliar country now and didn't know which way to turn. He was crossing a big flat field when he spied a farm house with a huge red barn beside it. Usually he avoided farm houses, but now this seemed the only possible refuge. On the far side of

75

the field the pack was streaming over the stone wall,
the riders just behind them. Directly before him was a
barbed-wire fence.

With one final effort Robbut made a long spring, his
forelegs stretched out straight in front, his hindlegs
stretched out behind, and shot cleanly between the wires
—all but his tail.

That pestiferous nuisance managed to get itself caught
on the barbs and there he hung, while the racing Hounds
burst into an exultant clamor. While the whole Hunt
came thundering across the field Robbut struggled and
fought and scrambled. With the leading Hound only a
few feet away he gave one last frantic yank and pulled

loose, leaving another couple of handfuls of orange fur
dangling from the wire.

He scuttled across the road with the pack on his very
heels, while the riders raced for a gate and came roaring
down the road. The barn door was open and Robbut
was making for that when he spied, in the stone foundation, one small hole — just about his size. Without

losing a step he swerved his course slightly, made one last despairing leap and shot cleanly through the hole into the cool darkness. So close had the leading Hound been that he crashed into the foundation at the same moment that Robbut hit the ground inside.

Fortunately there were no other openings and the hole that had saved him was far too small for a Hound to get through, although most of the pack tried to do so, all at the same time. They fought and yapped and scratched at the hole, but the stonework was strong and Robbut, for the moment, was safe. It was just in time too, for he was so exhausted that he just lay where he fell, almost unconscious of the confusion raging outside.

Of this there was a great deal.

The Hounds who were not scratching at the foundation began enthusiastically to hunt the Farmer's

poultry and in a few seconds managed to kill a Turkey, three Ducks, and seven Chickens. One Hound fell down the well while several others chased the Farmer's Cat up a tree.

Then the entire Swallowtail Hunt came piling into the barnyard, adding to the racket and confusion. What with the milling horses, the shouting riders, and the frantic blowing of the Huntsman's horn, two Cows broke loose and were wildly chased over the hill by the rest of the pack.

At this moment the Farmer, his Dog, and two sons arrived on the scene and the tumult doubled. The Dog was a large mongrel, mostly Mastiff, who tore into the Swallowtail Pack like an avenging angel, or, more properly, like an avenging devil. The Farmer was armed with a pitchfork and his two stout sons wielded hoes right lustily.

Over the screaming of the Hounds and the shouts of the riders the Huntsman tried to explain to the Farmer that a Fox had gone to earth under the barn. But the Farmer was not interested in Foxes and still less in Huntsmen.

"Well, if he's in there he stays there," he roared. He jammed a stone into the hole and went back to clubbing Dogs, with an occasional whack at such Horses as got in his way.

It was a riotous and thoroughly unpleasant half hour before the Hounds had been rounded up and quieted, the escaped Cows recaptured, the Hound rescued from the well, and the Cat from the tree. The damages were paid for, a passing motorist was persuaded to transport the more seriously damaged Hounds, and the Swallowtail Hunt, with its limping pack, straggled off homeward.

Through it all Robbut slept, in a coma of exhaustion.

8. Humility

Rᴏʙʙᴜᴛ never did know how long he was shut up under the barn. It might have been a day and a night or three days and nights. It was so dark in there that it was difficult to tell when it was night and when

81

it was day. He lost all track of time and didn't especially care, he was too exhausted and miserable.

His feet were worn and scratched and bruised. He ached in every joint and muscle. His head throbbed, and as for that tail—it seemed just one great attached pain. After the Hounds left he slept for a long, long time, he didn't know how long.

When he waked the ache in his head seemed to have transferred itself to his stomach, and he realized that he was starving hungry—and thirsty. Groaning at every move, he poked around a bit and found a small pile of grain which had sifted through the barn floor. This proved most nourishing, but made him still more thirsty, and there was no sign of water anywhere under the dry and dusty barn.

He went to sleep again and again didn't know for how long. This time when he woke he felt a little stronger, but even thirstier. It was impossible to face another bite of grain without a drink.

Actually, it was late afternoon of the day following the hunt when the Farmer, crossing the barnyard, happened to notice the stone still jammed into the hole. He had forgotten it in the excitement and now hastily pulled it out. "Don't want nothing dying under there," he muttered. "That *would* be a sweet mess." He sniffed at the hole and then grunted, "Don't believe nothing went in there anyhow. *Them hunters!*"

Even though it was a gray and drizzly evening the sudden light from the hole, after all the darkness, was almost blinding. It made Robbut's head ache again and the sound and smell of the cool rain almost drove him wild. He could just picture it settling in big silvery drops on the clover leaves. What wouldn't he give to bury his face in a cool, green clump of clover and lick off the raindrops! He certainly would give this tail, or a dozen like it.

But the previous day's terrifying experience had taught him a little caution—even for a Rabbit, so he took another nap, waiting for night to come.

It must have been almost midnight when he woke. Everything was quiet except for the drip of the rain, so with many groans and agonizing pains he managed to scramble up to the hole in the foundation. The effort almost exhausted him, but the cool drizzle was wonderfully refreshing. He held his face up to the sky and let the rain fall on it and trickle into his mouth. He licked the blessed wetness from his lips and paws, feeling better with every drop.

The farm house was all dark; from the barn came the heavy breathing of the Cows and Horses. Robbut felt fairly sure that the Farmer's Dog was slumbering soundly beside the kitchen range, so he hopped down and quietly made his way across the barnyard to the gate. Every step was agonizing; the once proud tail dragged

along behind him, gathering up mud and barnyard litter.

He crossed the road into a hayfield and soon found a thick patch of clover. He plunged his face into it and licked and licked up the cool raindrops. He ate quantities of the sweet fresh clover and felt still better. Not that he felt *good* by any means; every joint and muscle still ached, each step hurt his feet—and as for that tail! It was like being hitched to a heavy sandbag, and not a very clean or pleasant sandbag.

It was clear too that he was hopelessly lost. This was completely strange country, there were no familiar landmarks, he had no idea in which direction home lay. If

the moon or stars had been out they might have helped
as guides, but they were not. The night was pitch black
and the drizzle was turning to a heavy rain. There was
nothing to do but wait for daylight.

Robbut managed to get across the hayfield and creep
under a heavy bush. He remembered Foxy's proud boast
about the usefulness of his tail and tried to curl it over
his paws and bury his nose in it. But the tail was not soft

or fluffy or warm. It was cold and muddy and wet, and the trash it had picked up in the barnyard did not make it a pleasant place in which to bury one's nose.

Robbut said his prayers and then added, "And *please*, if I ever get back to the Little Man, *please* let me have my own little old tail back again and I'll never want any other." Then he went to sleep.

When he waked in the morning the rain had stopped and a thin sunlight was some comfort. Some, but not much, for the cold and wetness of the night had so stiffened him up that every movement brought a groan of pain. He ate some clover, licked up a lot of dew, and started slowly hopping along the hedgerow. He thought that if he kept the sun on his left he would be going toward home, but wasn't sure.

He came to a patch of woods and couldn't decide whether to go through or around it. Ordinarily he wouldn't have given it a thought, but with this awful tail dragging heavily along behind him he had to think of such things.

He chose to go through the woods, which was fortunate, for he had scarcely entered when he saw the tan gleam of a large, familiar Animal. He recognized it as the Red Deer who lived just across the river from the hill, a Deer whom he had known ever since he could remember.

At this moment the dragging tail caught in a briar

bush and Robbut, too tired to struggle further, called
weakly, "Oh, Buck, *please* help me. It's me, Robbut the
Rabbit."

The Deer twitched around quickly and cautiously approached. "Well, *well*," he said wonderingly, "it does *look* like Robbut, in a way, but what's that horrible thing you're dragging along behind you? It looks like it might have been a Fox's tail—once."

"It was—it is," Robbut sighed. "Oh, Buck, *please* help me get home!" Then he fainted away.

When Robbut came to, the Deer was lying beside him, his forelegs neatly tucked under his chest, his jaws moving slightly as he placidly chewed his cud. "Feeling any better?" he asked.

"I—I don't know," Robbut moaned. "I just feel terrible. I wish I was home."

"Well," said the Deer briskly, "let's do something about it. First gather yourself together and see if you can't pull that silly tail out of the briars. Then get up on my back, just forward of the shoulders. Put your legs on each side of my neck and hold on. I'll go gently. Come now, heave away."

Robbut heaved away with all the strength he had left. He pulled and yanked and scrambled, groaning with pain. Finally, with a terrible twinge, the tail pulled loose, leaving most of its remaining fur dangling from the briar bush. Robbut scrambled up and settled himself on the Deer's neck.

"Good," said the Deer, "very well done—for a Rabbit. Now hold on tight."

He carefully got to his feet and started off at a slow walk. Robbut found no trouble in staying on, in fact the gentle rocking motion soon became most restful. After they emerged from the woods the warm sun dried him out and baked some of the soreness from his muscles. He felt well enough to talk and told the Deer all about his various new tails and of his chase by the Swallowtail Hunt.

"Well, of all the idiotic things I've ever heard," the Deer snorted, "that's the most idiotic—even for a Rabbit. What's wrong with your own tail anyway? Why, look at mine. It's not much bigger than yours—in proportion, but you never heard of *me* wanting a new tail. A fine fix I'd be in racing around the woods with a Horse's tail, or even a Cow's tail. But I suppose some people never learn anything—especially Rabbits."

"I have," Robbut said meekly. "If I once get home and get my own tail back again, I'll never, *never*, want another."

"I'll believe *that*," the Deer chuckled, "when Crows sing like Mockingbirds."

He increased his pace and soon Robbut began to sight familiar landmarks. They went down a long hill and he could see the river shining in the sun.

"I'll take you across the ford," the Deer said when they had reached the stream, "but I'm not going on the other side. There have been some annoying Dogs there

89

lately. You can make it up the hill all right, can't you?"

"Yes, thank you," Robbut answered, "I'm sure I can now."

The Deer stepped daintily across the shallow ford and bent his neck down when they reached the near shore. Robbut slipped off onto the bank and tried to thank him, but the Deer only laughed and splashed back across the stream. As he neared the far bank his beautiful little white flag of a tail flicked up as though signaling a good-by, then he vanished into the bushes.

"My," Robbut said admiringly. "His tail *isn't* much bigger than mine, and it's *so* untroublesome." Then he began the painful climb up through the brushy clearing, his useless, bedraggled, aching Fox's tail dragging along behind him.

The Little Old Man chuckled as he answered Robbut's feeble knock, but when he saw his sad condition became most concerned and kindly. He at once put the stone crock on the stove to heat and then looked Robbut over carefully.

"Well, *well*," he cried, "this seems to have been the worst choice of all. You *are* a mess. Now, I should say the first thing is to rid you of this unsavory encumbrance that you're dragging around. Then a bowl of hot soup

91

and then sleep—lots of it. Come now, hop up on the table."

But Robbut wasn't able to hop up on the table and had to be lifted up. While the Little Man bustled around Robbut crouched there with his forepaws over his eyes. His paws seemed hot, yet he was having fits of shivering. "Feverish," the Little Man said, fetching the stone crock. "We'll fix that up too."

Robbut smelled the familiar odor and then slowly, miraculously, he felt the pain and the heavy dragging weight of the Fox's tail disappear. A moment later the Little Man slapped him gently on the back and cried, "There you are, the same old tail, better than ever. And more welcome than ever, I'll bet."

Painful though it was, Robbut stretched his neck as far as he could and twisted his head as far as he could. He was just able to catch a glimpse of his own little old tufty, cottony tail, but the relief and effort were too much. He gave a deep sigh and keeled over on the table.

He was dimly aware of being picked up and laid gently in the bunk. His head sank into the soft pillow and he felt the warm quilt being drawn over him. Then he didn't know anything more.

It must have been late the next afternoon when Robbut woke again, for the rays of warm sun that poured

in the little windows were almost level. Very, very carefully he stretched each limb and joint and was overjoyed
to find all the soreness and stiffness completely gone. He
sighed a great sigh of happiness, which caused the Little
Old Man to look up from his book.

"Well," he said, "and how do you feel now—better?
And what would you think of a good hot bowl of pea-
vine soup—good?"

"Wonderful!" Robbut cried, leaping out of bed.

He was a bit weak and shaky, but otherwise felt fine.
The finest thing of all was the lack of that dragging
weight on his rear end. He almost felt as though he
were floating. He wanted to kick up his heels and make
long soaring leaps over rocks and bushes. He felt cautiously around and was reassured by the neat firm feeling of his little old tufty tail.

"I guess I've got about the finest tail in the world," he
said happily.

"I guess you have—for a Rabbit," the Little Old Man
laughed. "Now sit on it and eat your soup." Robbut
lapped up his soup in almost no time and settled back
with a contented sigh.

"Now," said the Little Man, "get along home with you.
Your parents are worried. Do you realize that you've
been gone four nights?"

"No—I didn't," Robbut admitted. "It all seems like
a bad dream—sort of."

Then, after a thoughtful silence, he said, "There's one thing I'd like to do though, before I go, if you don't mind."

"Help yourself," the Little Man said.

Robbut drew a stool over to the stove and climbed up on it. He took off one stove lid and looked for some time at the glowing coals. Then he slid the little stone crock over, dumped it into the fire and quickly put back the lid. There was a short roaring and sizzling of flames, a little smoke puffed through the cracks of the stove, and then the fire died down again. The room was filled with that strange but not unpleasant odor.

"Well, that's that," laughed the Little Old Man, holding the door open. "At last you seem to have gotten a little sense—for a Rabbit. But remember, if you don't like your tail now there's nothing I can do about it."

"That's all right with me," Robbut called back happily. "That suits me *fine*."

The Woodchuck was waddling up the path and Robbut soared over him in an exultant leap.

"Humph," the Woodchuck snorted. "Some people are never satisfied."

"*I* am," Robbut laughed. "I am for all time." And he galloped down through the sunset toward home.

94